Onstage & Backstage

AT THE NIGHT OWL THEATER

WRITTEN BY Ann Hayes

ILLUSTRATED BY Karmen Thompson

Harcourt Brace & Company

San Diego   New York   London

Special thanks to Patti McFerran, Geri Busse,
Howard Bashinski, Cindy Lair, Hal Landem,
Mary Ann Nitchie, J. P. Osnes, Eloise Pelton,
and Meg Leighton for their advice and support

—A. H. & K. T.

Library of Congress Cataloging-in-Publication Data
Hayes, Ann.
Onstage and backstage/written by Ann Hayes;
illustrated by Karmen Thompson.
p. cm.
Summary: Describes the work done by various people—the director,
stage manager, set designer, actors, and others—involved in putting
on the play "Cinderella."
ISBN 0-15-200782-2
1. Theater—Production and direction—Juvenile literature.
[1. Theater—Production and direction.]
I. Thompson, Karmen, ill.   II. Title.
PN2053.H34   1997
792'.023—dc20   96-19934

First edition

F E D C B A

Printed in Singapore

The illustrations in this book were done
in watercolor on Crescent watercolor board.
The display type was hand-lettered by Georgia Deaver.
The text type was set in Simoncini Garamond by
Harcourt Brace & Company
Photocomposition Center, San Diego, California.
Color separations by Bright Arts, Ltd., Singapore
Printed and bound by Tien Wah Press, Singapore
This book was printed on totally chlorine-free
Nymolla Matte Art paper.
Production supervision by Stanley Redfern
Designed by Lori McThomas Buley

For our children—Andy Goodman, Tom Goodman,
Keith Effenberger, and Pauli Chapman—who have inspired
us and continue to cheer us on

—A. H. & K. T.

Duffy looks at his calendar and counts the days. *Cinderella* opens in just four weeks, and there's so much to do! Actors must be chosen, lines must be learned, costumes must be sewn, and sets must be built. It must all come together by opening night. How will everything get done?

Duffy is the director, and his first job is to select the cast. He glances at his watch. Ten o'clock—time for auditions to begin. As he listens to actors read from the script, he thinks about how to match them up with the characters in *Cinderella*. Some actors will be called back to read again. Then Duffy will cast the play.

A few days after the cast is chosen, Duffy brings everyone together for the read-through. They read the script out loud from beginning to end so the actors can get to know their characters and how the play unfolds.

After they read the entire play, Duffy introduces Biggs. "Our

stage manager, Biggs, is my partner," he says. "While I sit out front watching you rehearse, she takes care of everything onstage and backstage." Biggs keeps copies of the script, set plans, and rehearsal schedules in a fat notebook. The actors call it Biggs's Big Book.

During the first week of rehearsals, Duffy blocks all the scenes in the play so the actors know where to move on the stage. The stepmother and stepsisters will stand at center stage and order Cinderella about as they dress for the ball.

"Cinderella, fetch my gloves!"

"Cinderella, fetch my fan!"

"Cinderella, fetch my jewels!"

Duffy's sketch shows Cinderella where she should go to obey their commands.

"Please mark your script so you memorize your stage directions along with your lines. And be sure to learn your cues," says Duffy. "Pretty soon you'll know the whole play by heart."

As soon as the cast has been selected, Minnie, the publicity director, begins spreading the news about the play—when it is, where it is, and how to get tickets. Publicity photos are taken. Press releases are sent to newspapers and radio stations. Posters are printed and hung around town. The cast and crew tell their friends, "Don't miss *Cinderella* at the Night Owl Theater!"

Boris, the set designer, has made color sketches of the sets to show how the stage will be dressed for each scene.

The stage crew saws and hammers, making lots of noise as they follow Boris's plans. They build light wooden frames that they cover with cloth and paint to look like the walls of Cinderella's kitchen. The pumpkin coach is fitted with rollers so it can travel across the stage. Boris and his assistant paint a mural of the ballroom scene on a cloth drop that can be raised and lowered from the fly loft overhead.

Pringle, who runs the costume shop, measures the actors for their costumes and checks the Night Owl Theater's storage closet for treasures. There she finds gowns, waistcoats, blouses, and britches for the lords, ladies, and village folk. Vanya and Misha, her helpers, stitch Cinderella's magnificent ball gown, which is brand-new. Wanda creates fancy wigs.

Gepetto, the prop master, and his assistant, Tinker, have a long list of the props needed for the play. They find a pretty cage for the white mice in the Night Owl's prop room. Three hand mirrors turn up at a neighborhood garage sale. They buy a teakettle and a tea set at the thrift shop around the corner. A skilled craftsman, Gepetto makes a reed broom, a magic wand, and a papier-mâché pumpkin by hand.

With just two weeks left before opening night, rehearsals are in full swing. The actors have learned their lines by heart.

"We are off book," Duffy says with a touch of pride. "Now you can really begin to act!" He and the actors talk about how to bring the characters to life onstage.

"Cinderella, as you sweep the hearth, you dream of going to the ball. How can you show that?"

"I could dance with the broom—as if it were the prince—like this?"

"Godmother, suddenly you must change a pumpkin into a coach, rats into footmen, and rags into a beautiful gown. You are out of practice. How do you feel?"

"I'm flustered! Let's see. I could thumb through my book of magic spells—like this?"

Widget sits at Duffy's side and follows the script. He is ready to prompt the actors, just in case.

Chloe, an expert choreographer, has come to teach the actors the waltz for the ballroom scene. The ladies wear practice skirts so they can get used to dancing in long, billowy dresses. After all have learned the basic step, they pair up and try waltzing. At first they teeter and trip, but soon they swirl gracefully around the stage.

Toby and Tanny sit in the control booth at the back of the theater.

Toby, the lighting engineer, uses dimmers to make lights fade and brighten smoothly. He can cast shadows, create a sunset, light a lamp, or blacken the entire stage.

Tanny, the sound engineer, has recorded the singing of a teakettle, the striking of a clock, the squeaking of mice, and the music of a waltz all onto one tape. He makes sure the audience will hear each sound at exactly the right moment.

Opening night is less than one week away, and technical rehearsals have begun.

The stage crew practices changes of scene. Light and sound effects are rehearsed until they are perfectly timed to the action of the play. From her spot in the wings, Biggs runs the show. Through the intercom, she gives cues to everyone onstage, backstage, and in the control booth.

At the dress rehearsal, everything is set up exactly as it will be on opening night. The sets are complete. The actors are fully costumed. Even if something goes wrong, the play must not stop.

Plenty does go wrong! The pumpkin coach gets stuck; a spotlight burns out; the prince trips.

All through the play, Duffy scribbles notes. When the rehearsal is over, cast and crew listen patiently to his comments. "Don't worry, kids," he says. "A bad dress rehearsal means good luck on opening night. We'll get it right tomorrow."

It's opening night, and the show begins in just one hour. The actors get ready in the dressing room. Some do stretches. Others recite tongue twisters like "Red leather, yellow leather" to warm up their voices and to ease the jitters. Pringle brings armloads of freshly ironed costumes.

Through the intercom in the wings, Biggs announces: "Thirty minutes to curtain."

The ladies step into their gowns and don their wigs. Cinderella

The curtain opens.

"Cinderella, fetch my jewels!"

 "You must be home by the stroke of midnight."

puts on the rags she wears in the first act. Wanda adds final touches to the actors' makeup.

From the control booth, Toby watches the audience enter, then presses the intercom switch. "It's going to be a full house, Biggs!" he says.

Biggs switches the intercom over to the dressing room. "It's a full house. Five minutes to curtain. Break a leg, everyone!" Then, switching back to Toby: "House down." The house lights dim.

 "It's a perfect fit. Our search is over!"

The Night Owl Theater rocks with applause. *Cinderella* is a smash! The actors return, one by one, until everyone stands together. Duffy and Biggs join them onstage.

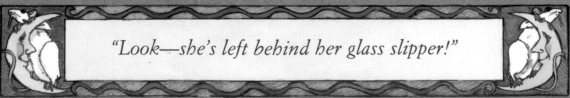

"Look—she's left behind her glass slipper!"

Then they all take a bow . . . and another . . . and another. After three curtain calls, the stage lights dim. Onstage and backstage, the cast and crew rejoice!

Theater Words

audition *(noun)*   A short performance to show or test the ability of an actor. Also called a tryout.

backstage   The part of the stage that is hidden from the audience, including the areas on either side and in back.

block *(verb)*   To map out the movements of actors on the stage.

"Break a leg!"   A theater expression for "Good luck!"

cast *(noun)*   The actors in a play.

cast *(verb)*   To choose actors for the parts in a play.

character   A person in a play who is portrayed by an actor.

choreographer   One who plans movements, such as dances or sword fights, and teaches them to actors.

crew   A team that does one type of work, such as building or moving scenery.

cue   A signal that tells an actor when to speak or move.

curtain call   An appearance onstage after a play to respond to the applause of the audience.

director   One who works closely with actors and designers to create a play according to his or her interpretation.

dress rehearsal   A full rehearsal, with actors in costume and sets in place, that occurs shortly before opening night.

drop *(noun)*   A curtain without folds that hangs from the fly loft and is often painted to depict a background scene.

fly loft   The area high above the stage from which scenery can be raised and lowered.

house   The auditorium in front of the stage where the audience sits.

lines   The words an actor speaks in a play.

off book   The point at which actors have memorized their lines and no longer need to refer to the script.

onstage   The acting area of the stage, visible to the audience.

opening night   The first performance of a play.

prompt *(verb)*   To remind an actor of his or her lines.

prop   A movable object that is placed or used in a set, not including costumes or scenery.

read-through	A gathering of the cast to read an entire script out loud.
rehearsal	A practice performance.
scene	A section of a play, defined by continuous action.
script	The written text of a play.
set (*noun*)	The acting area, complete with scenery and props.
set designer	One who researches and designs sets and scenery.
stage directions	Instructions that tell actors where to move on the stage during a performance.
stage manager	An assistant to the director who oversees all aspects of a production, including rehearsals, props, and technical elements.
technical rehearsal	A rehearsal during which sound cues, light cues, and set changes are practiced.
wings	Side pieces used as scenery and to conceal the actors waiting to go onstage.